WILD BABIES

Nan Richardson &
Catherine Chermayeff
An Umbra Editions Book

WILD BABIES

CHRONICLE BOOKS

SAN FRANCISCO

Printed in Hong Kong.

Book and cover design: Vanessa Ryan
Edited by Nan Richardson and Catherine Chermayeff
Consulting Editor: Les Kaufman

Library of Congress Cataloging-in-Publication Data
Wild babies / by Nan Richardson and
Catherine Chermayeff: text by Nan Richardson.
p. cm.
ISBN 0-8118-0477-1
1. Animals--Infancy--Pictorial works. I. Richardson, Nan.
II. Catherine Chermayeff
QL763.W54 1994
591.3'9'0222--dc20   93-2330
                                       CIP

Distributed in Canada by Raincoast Books,
112 East Third Avenue, Vancouver, B.C. V5T 1C8

10 9 8 7 6 5 4 3 2 1

An Umbra Editions, Inc., Book

Umbra Editions, Inc.
145 Avenue of the Americas
New York, New York 10013

Chronicle Books
275 Fifth St.
San Francisco, CA 94103

CONTENTS

INTRODUCTION

Flying, crawling, swimming, and walking on this earth are over one million known species of animals: birds and reptiles, fish and insects, mammals and more. Aside from the ubiquitous and lowly protozoa, this plenitude of creatures all derives from the classic coincidence of the egg with its necessary counterpart, the spermatozoa. But from this common denominator, life from conception to birth to childhood and beyond is limitlessly varied. Nowhere is this elegant variation so apparent than in the gamut of parent-child relationships, from blood and thunder to tender nurturing, from indifference to obsession. One of our more primitive relatives, the Nile crocodile, for example, takes enormous care with her newborn, vigilantly waiting for the first signs of hatching and ferrying the squiggly young to the river's edge in her mouth, chirping to them as she scuttles back and forth. Nature's hormonal clock is also at work for a mother bear, who sinks into twilight sleep in autumn and gives birth to tiny cubs in snowy January, nursing them while she dozes the rest of the winter away. But mother love is not the only chemically induced reaction to parenting.

Male participation in child-rearing is by no means uncommon in the wild—in fact, quite the reverse. The male seahorse has evolved a special pouch almost like a surrogate womb for carrying the eggs transferred to him by the female until the moment of birth. Male baboons (not necessarily fathers of the infants) regularly serve as baby-sitters, as mothers go off for a meal or a social visit, several times a day. Of course, hardly all is sweetness and altruism. Some primates show a nature redder in tooth and claw. After fights between groups of langur monkeys, the victors may kill the offspring of the vanquished in a bloodbath of infanticide. From an evolutionary perspective, it may not be just gratuitous violence, for afterward the females quickly come into estrus, ready to mate with their new lords. Even the young can possess a special ferocity; the sand tiger sharks' special form of incest involves devouring their siblings in the womb. Nature teems with the odd and impossible, from the hornbills that immure female and offspring in a tomblike nest to the vaquero frog males, several of which swallow one female's eggs, later releasing the offspring by regurgitation. Bonds between parent and child may be cemented through sound, as in the incessant chittering and cooing between infant baboons and their parents, or through sight, as the famous ethnologist Konrad Lorenz proved when he hatched goose eggs himself. The baby goslings that followed him in a line to the pond clearly regarded him as their mother, source of food and comfort. An old primitive magic is at work here, with instincts as irresistible as the sexual. In fact, erotic behavior may be a variation on the vocabulary of parent-child bonds: kissing is said to have been a relic of a parent's feeding children from the mouth, and kneading and stroking is a seamless part of the repertoire of offering the mother's breast. But whatever its source, animal parenting teaches us that domesticated, "civilized" humankind unconsciously is not so very different from other mammals, and that whatever morality human beings have invented for ourselves, we all dance, like the animals, to some higher lexicon of order.

The armadillo's jump reflex when startled gives it a defense mechanism from birth, in spite of the seemingly weighty shell.

JACK-IN-THE-BOX

Equipped with a suit of armor like some medieval knight, the nine-banded armadillo boasts of a native range from Argentina to the United States. Nocturnal in summer, it can be seen surfacing at dusk to lick up anthills as single-mindedly as a child with a double-fudge ice cream cone. Armadillos are unique in giving birth to almost-identical quadruplets, all of the same sex. Produced by a four-way split of a single fertilized egg, the carbon-copy embryos are conceived in the fall but spend three months in "cold storage" before they attach to the uterus and begin to grow. Sometimes the delay can extend as long as twenty months—making armadillo gestation as long as the elephant's. The reason for this is probably an evolutionary adjustment so that the young won't be born at the beginning of winter, when food is scarce. Babies are normally born around February—in the season that gives them the best chance for survival—sporting a soft, light, leathery, flexible skin. This will not stiffen until the armadillo reaches full size, assuring a perfect fit throughout life.

THE MUD BATH

*Hunted because of
its abundant, highly
prized flesh and
hide (said by native
people to taste like
pork and make
excellent soup),
the baby hippo has
a serious predator
with which to
contend—man.*

Hippopotomidae (and their cousins, the pygmy hippos) spend a great deal of their life in water; on land their sensitive slate-brown skin would get dry and scaly. More importantly, their legs would cease to support their ponderous weight. Aquatic females, in particular, need elasticity to support the tremendous bulk of their calves— which at birth, after 240 days of gestation, may weigh up to 100 pounds. Young hippos can swim before they can walk and can nurse underwater. Cows are devoted to their calves, and on a sunny African afternoon at the mud wallow, the joyous splashing may be a youngster's scramble onto the mother's back to sun while she floats in the river. An added benefit in this perch for the baby hippo is protection from crocodiles, but paradoxically, the noise may draw the attention of the hippo's two-legged predator, man, to the river's edge.

Celebrated in song and story for their faithfulness, geese are also among those birds who care for their young for a full year. Romance for the goose begins early, before goslings reach sexual maturity. First, a young male has to impress a female and lure her away from her protective family. When she departs with him, a long "engagement" period precedes actual mating. At that time, the female makes a depression with her beak and sweeps together a nest of grass and moss on a foundation of sticks. Once she has laid the eggs, she yanks out beakfuls of breast down to bare her swollen brood-spot, pressing her chest against the cool eggs to further the incubation. The gander stands sentry at the nest for a month; then, within twenty-four hours of hatching, he leads the goslings all in a row from the nest to water, while the female brings up the rear. Both guard their offspring as they learn to swim, dive, and feed. By the time the goslings are eight weeks old, they are twenty-five times their birth weight and ready for the big flight south.

Even the migration flight of the wild geese, with their deeply musical honking while in perfect V-formation flight, is done en famille.

PERFECT PAIRINGS

RED IN TOOTH AND CLAW

Infanticide is practiced by many mammal species, including the silver-haired langur.

Langurs are long-tailed, black-faced monkeys common on the Indian subcontinent. Troops of up to sixty individuals are composed of related females and offspring, together with only one breeding male. Infants are fussed over and freely passed from hand to hand, with each female getting her chance to pat the baby. If an infant is female she will eventually be accepted into the troop, but male adolescent offspring have to leave home. They form teenage gangs, and later bachelor bands that roam at will, attacking the stable troops in their range. These border battles are fought more with screaming and chasing than with actual violence, and the resident male, backed by his harem, often repulses the invaders. But if the bachelors manage to oust him, they will snatch infants from their mothers and destroy them. This has the effect of bringing females into heat again and allowing the usurper to establish his own line. Nevertheless, a pregnant female resorts to tricks to keep her unborn young, behaving as though she is in estrus and offering herself to the new ruler, who mates with her. Then when her infant is born, the ruler believes it to be his own and allows it to live.

Most felines are solitary creatures. Lions, however, are social cats, to the benefit of the cubs.

KITTY CLUBS

Lions live in prides, the females being the core of these groups, with cubs and adult males coming and going. Females in a pride tend to be related to one another, and they even take turns nursing one another's cubs. Lion cubs are born three and a half months after the lioness is impregnated. Normally, a female gives birth to not more than three cubs. Their chances of survival are enhanced if more than one lioness in a pride has a litter, so they will share nursing duties. Lion cubs grow up surrounded by adults. Cubs play all day long among themselves and with the adults. They pummel the different members of the pride with their paws, biting their tails, licking their faces, and pulling their hair. Males are less patient with the cubs—especially those playing when the males are asleep—than are the females, and sometimes sting the cubs with the ends of their tails, so as to be left alone.

Conceptions peak in number among African rhinos during the rainy season, and birth follows a leisurely sixteen months after, with intervals between calves lasting about three years. These near-sighted herbivores bear their first young at six to eight years, and a single offspring is the rule. Mothers seek secluded places to give birth, and the newborn calves, wobbling quickly to their feet to give suck, are small (130 pounds) relative to their two-ton mothers. In about three days, the calf accompanies its mother to forage, running in front of her where she can watch for predators. The white rhino mother also straddles her calf protectively if danger threatens. Mothers and calves, along with other young females, feed across favored ranges of about eight square miles, greeting each other by rubbing noses and by engaging in playful wrestling matches. These most sociable of rhinos are mild and inoffensive, even timid, by nature. When frightened they take up a defensive formation, facing outward with rumps pressed together, protecting the calves in the center. Effective against lions, it is sadly useless against humans, and the white rhino's struggle for survival continues.

THE SHY UNICORN

Ceratotherium simum, *better known as the white rhino, has been making a comeback in South Africa, despite the demand for its horn.*

EGGS IN ONE BASKET

Parenthood for the largest birds in the world (standing over eight feet tall) begins with a very large egg.

With a flutter of tail feathers, the usually fleet-footed female ostriches (at 43 mph, the speediest two-legged creatures on earth) wiggle and shrug in the dry dust until they have carved out a comfortable hollow. Between them, they will lay up to forty giant eggs in the nest, but there is only room for the dominant hen to incubate half. So she lays her own eggs in the protected center, and rolls any uncomfortable extra eggs out towards the edges. Then she sits for a long, hot, fifty days, vigorously defending the nest. As the eggs warm, she turns them to cool her own feverish "brooding spot," that temporarily defeathered area towards the middle of the breast. The chicks are born, fully feathered and with shell bits still sticking to their rump as they run around briskly. If a predator approaches, the mother will put on astonishing performances to protect her nest, fluttering lopsidedly across the ground, pretending to be wounded to distract the aggressor's attention away from her defenseless young. All of these oversized strategies for reproduction help insure the longevity of the big bird. Among the longest-living of all animals, an ostrich can reach the age of one hundred.

*Male snow monkeys
of the macaque
genus are noted for
their care and use
of babies in social
interactions.*

ONE CARD STUD

Groups huddle together in the forest, arms over each other's shoulders, teeth chattering, lips smacking, grimacing, and purring while they hold a week-old infant upside down admiringly. After a few minutes the interaction ends and the bewildered infant is absentmindedly groomed by a lone male. The babies are passive participants in this elaborate game, and if none are around, a dead infant or even an inanimate object has been known to substitute. The use of babies as poker chips stems from the fact that macaque groups have a matrilineal core; females hold hierarchical rank, and kinship to them opens the possibility of entry to the group. A male's bid for acceptance can succeed through his caretaking responsibility for an infant, as he develops ties with other males who are related to the same infant. The use of babies as buffers is also common. In a fight a male might pick up an infant and hold it out as a stop sign to an aggressor. Appeased, the attacker abandons his threat and joins the male in huddling over the baby. The net effect of all this male attention is not only infant nurturing but also a tension-free social environment.

Inverting the normal
gravitational
harmonies, bats
give birth upside
down, hanging
by feet and thumb.

RECEIVING BLANKETS

By bending her tail and body slightly in an arc, the mother bat forms a capacious apron with which to catch her emergent young. In a half an hour, labor is over, and the contractions soon force the placenta out of the uterus. Born tail first, blind, and naked, the bat baby actually helps pull itself out of the womb. It immediately bites onto a teat, as the mother busies herself cutting the umbilical cord and downing the afterbirth. Females give birth to one pup a year, and they sometimes carry even the young that are able to fly (when the pup weighs as much as two-thirds of the mother's weight). In some species, like the gray bat, mothers deposit their newborns in a nursery of thousands and return only two times daily to feed them. The intense clustering seems to stabilize the naked infant's body temperature and provides a secure spot while the mother forages. In a remarkable display of motherly love, 85 percent of the time these bat mothers are able to locate their own infant immediately among the densely packed horde.

While thousands of sterile female honey bees serve the state as workers and soldiers, the entire apparatus has one purpose: to produce progeny—fertilized eggs developing into females and a small amount of unfertilized eggs developing into males. The females care for the larvae in a gigantic nursery, feeding them a white paste full of hormones and eventually sending them out to found a new state. The individual bee's different duties in this so-called "republic of love" change in the course of her forty-two-day life. Their call to duty sounds two days after hatching, when the female bee already becomes a baby-sitter, feeding future workers and drones "worker jelly," while the one larva chosen as the next queen receives a daily dose of "royal jelly." A week later the bee is promoted to general housework, excreting wax and kneading it into honeycombs, as well as standing guard at the hive entrance. After this she travels out as a forager, bringing home nectar, pollen, water, and other necessities to feed the endless supply of new baby bees that the pulpous queen, engorged on her jelly diet, is diligently producing.

FIFTY THOUSAND VIRGINS

The vast order called Hymenoptera *("membranous wings") is an elaborate structure to support a single queen bee and her offspring, numbering two thousand eggs per day.*

Australia's sleepy-
eyed little tourist
attraction gives birth
about once every
other year to a
peanut-sized koala
cub, weighing less
than a quarter ounce.

UPSIDE DOWN AND DOWN UNDER

As with its marsupial cousin on the evolutionary tree, the kangaroo, the newborn koala has to immediately perform a survival feat and climb from the birth canal up the mother's body to her nipples. After nursing for five months, spending time between meals in the maternal pouch, the diet of mother's milk is replaced by a mixture of semidigested eucalyptus leaves. These leaves are poisonous for all mammals except koalas, whose stomachs are equipped with special microbial enzymes to break down the poisons. The baby koala's system adapts to this diet by licking up the still-live enzymes from his mother's rear end, explaining the mystery of the posterior pouch placement. When, after about eight months, the accommodations get too snug, the infant rides piggyback—while another year goes by before it reaches the adult height of two feet and can fend for itself. With such a long, slow childhood (up to eighteen hours a day of it spent snoozing in the nook of a tree) the species has developed a way to double up production: koalas have a reproductive canal that allows one infant in the pouch while another is being born.

The sand shark's yellowish coloring is perfectly adapted for cruising the shadowy ocean floor, feeding at night on bottom-dwelling fish and the occasional lobster or unsuspecting crab. Sexually mature when they reach about six feet in length, females give birth to two baby sharks per litter in spite of the hundreds of tiny bean-sized eggs they release during the three-month pregnancy. The reason is that these two feed on the other eggs and even on younger embryos while still in the mother's womb. Because of this prebirth cannibalism, at the actual time of birth the remaining young are already three feet long. These cannibal offspring are none too picky about their next meal—one scientist reaching inside a freshly caught female was sharply bitten by the unborn sand shark fetus.

SIBLING RIVALRIES

The torpedo shape
of the tiger sand shark
knifing through
the tropical blue seas
is unmistakable,
as are the teeth—
noticeably long, thin,
icicle smooth,
and jaggedly sharp.

MADONNA OF THE SEA

Hairless and wrinkly, they were the sirens that lured mirage-struck sailors toward the shores and gave rise to the legend of the mermaids. At two thousand pounds and twelve feet long, the manatee made an oversized love object. The manatee's lazy days are spent snorting up a hundred pounds of water hyacinths and other tasty plants with its elephantlike mouth (on land, the manatee's closest cousins are the pachyderms). For female manatees a birth is an event, with a calf arriving about every three years, after a gestation period of fourteen months. Born in a bubble sac of amniotic fluid, the baby pricks it with his nose and, his mother gently pushing from behind, floats to the surface to take his first breath of air. For the next two years, the affectionate mother and child are inseparable, and a thumb-sized nipple under her flipper offers daily sustenance. When she's not busy with her own ten-course meals, mother sits up in the water clasping her infant to her breast between her flippers—a scene, worthy of a trecento master, that has earned her the sobriquet Madonna of the Sea.

FLEECE AND FEATHERS

The richly colored pheasant was part of the legendary booty of Jason and his Argonauts, who brought these exotic birds, along with the mythic Golden Fleece, from Asia to Greece.

On a bright spring day in the English countryside, the female pheasant builds her grounded nest in a hollow in the corn fields or on a bare spot in green cow pasture, lining it gently with weed stems, grasses, and a fine inner blanket of soft leaves and feathers. There she sits, immovable on her clutch of brown-olive eggs, getting her water from the morning dew that collects on her dark-green ruff, while the stalwart male stands guard during brooding. She often has company, though—other females with the same male as protector build their nests alongside, within his crowing area. Occasionally the cock also may take his turn at nesting, and often two hens will share the same nest. Both parents are at the nest when the chicks hatch. Once the chicks are clean and dry, the parents lead them to a safer haven. If a predator approaches, the parents will flutter noisily away as decoys, pretending to drag a broken wing to lure the fox or hawk away, while the chicks scatter and hide. When night falls, or if the weather turns chill, the mother hen extends her warming wings over them till balmy sun returns.

The agility of the mountain goat defies gravity, as only a few hours after birth a kid follows its mother along precipitous ledges or screes.

FROM COIGN TO COIGN

The family of *Caprinae*, or goat antelopes, ranges from hot deserts to alpine plateaus, and glacier cliffs to tropic forests. Not true goats, the mountain goat is a species that came to North America from Eurasia in an early Ice Age. With bodies built for snow climbing—flexible hoofs, compact, muscular torsos, short legs (poor for running but perfect for balance)—they spend much of life in lofty realms where few foes dare to follow. After the first heavy snows the mixed male and female flocks break up, moving from the woodland ranges. They winter over alone in mountainous areas, when living in a flock would be deadly, feeding on sparse grass, sedges, shrubs, and lichens. It is a hard time for the youngest among them, with heavy mortality rates. Come June, after a four-month gestation, short-tailed kids are born to their hundred-pound mothers in inaccessible rocky areas where the pregnant ewes have hidden before delivering. Each ewe's single kid per year is fully dressed in long, fluffy white underwool and leg "pantaloons." A month later they venture out of their cave hideaways to rejoin the flock in the upland meadows.

36

Short necked and stubby nosed, the donkey-sized tapir has a compact shape ideal for pushing through the dense undergrowth of the forest floor, using its sensitive proboscis to pull leaves and shoots within reach. The design extends to its eyes, small and recessed deep in the tough, hairless skin, where they are well protected from thorns. Apart from mothers with young, tapirs are solitary and shy, moving on a zig-zag course to feed, swimming and sleeping on the banks of rivers and lakes. Just before they give birth (after a 400-day pregnancy), mothers seek a secure lair in which to bear their single young (twins are rare). Whatever the species, the newborn tapir is dark reddish brown dappled with yellow and white stripes and spots. This is excellent camouflage in the mottled light and cool shade of the jungle undergrowth, as protection from its predators—the jaguar, tiger, and leopard. In six to eight months however, the pattern has vanished, and soon the tapir begins to travel on its own. Three short years will pass before it reaches sexual maturity—plenty of time to hone its survival skills, since it may live to the ripe age of thirty.

Proof positive that the continents were once connected, the stout, sturdy tapir ranges from Southeast Asia to South America.

CONTINENTAL DRIFT

*Looking like some
shaggy refugee from
the Pleistocene
Age, the musk ox
is the northernmost
hoofed animal.*

SHELTER FROM THE STORM

Inuit natives call them *oomingmak*, meaning "bearded one," for adults sport a six-inch deep brown coat (hardly useful for disguise but good for soaking up the Arctic sun) that makes them the furriest animals alive. When the spring tundra is brilliant with color and rich in food, the 800-pound female musk oxen give birth to their calves. Babies are born uniquely equipped for the treeless cold and icy winds, in a full overcoat of curly hair finer than cashmere. By the time winter comes, the calves have doubled in weight and are ready for the Arctic tempests. The herd assumes a curious defense posture born of the ages against predators and the cold blizzards from the north, showing their devotion to their offspring. Moving to high ground, they form a phalanx, horns out, with the calves in the center behind the adults' furry ramparts. When challenged by a predator, one male launches furious counter charges while the others close ranks behind. Such a strategy works well against wolves, but the musk oxens' loyalty to herd members didn't help them with man: only a 1917 Canadian edict saved them from extinction.

The name "lemur" means ghost, perhaps because of the animal's appearances and disappearances in the shadowy foliage of the forest. Habitually traveling in the trees but perfectly comfortable on the forest floor, smell is the lemur's most important faculty. They roam by night, grunting, whistling, and shrieking to each other as they smear their tails with secretions and wave them at opponents. While females (especially the ruffed lemur) have given birth to two or more infants at a time, lone offspring are more common. Babies are born almost hairless, eyes wide open, after a short (forty-eight hour) synchronized period of heat, resulting in a peak June birth rate. Born with disproportionately large heads, and clutching at the mother's abdominal fur, after three weeks the newborn has already moved to the mother's back. By five months weaning is completed and two months later the baby is living alone. "Alone" is a relative term among the lemurs, however; troops of up to thirty individuals range across sixty acres, and call out to each other sociably as they flit through the trees.

The island of Madagascar is a hothouse laboratory of lemur evolution, with 40 species developing from an ancestral primate 50 million years ago.

GHOSTS OF THE PAST

Over two thousand years ago, Pliny recorded that hedgehogs carried fruit impaled on their spines—a tale the Chinese believed as well.

PRICKLY PARENTING

Folk tales about the common hedgehog abound—that it sucks milk from sleeping cows, and is impervious to snakebite. But there is no need for fiction; fact is odd enough. Twelve species exist in Europe, Asia, and Africa, varying in size and shape but similar in many habits. One is the propensity of hedgehogs to coat their spines with saliva, flicking it on with their long tongues. Females give birth after breeding in May or September, preparing a nest in advance for four pale-pink naked young. Born with eyes and ears closed, they also have the characteristic spines—but they are buried beneath the skin, so that they do not damage the mother's birth canal. After birth, the extra fluid in their skin evaporates, allowing it to contract, and 150 white spines miraculously emerge. Within thirty-six hours the babies turn dark brown, and in two weeks they learn to roll up, a handy defense mechanism discouraging all but the most desperately hungry predators. After eight weeks, hedgehogs are ousted from the nest to fend for themselves. The summer's first litter has a distinct advantage over a second, with more time to build up fat before hibernating in winter.

Some 450 million years ago the supercontinent of Gondwanaland cupped the bottom of the globe. Over time, Australia floated free, inhabited by marsupials much like the two hundred species found there today. Among these survivors is the Tasmanian pademelon, which, like the kangaroo, wallaby, potoroo, and quokka, has distinct reproductive quirks. Prime among these is the tiny, hairless, embryonic state of its offspring. Without any assistance from the pademelon mother, the blind infant must make an arduous trek, pulling itself hair by hair, from the birth canal to the warm safety of the mother's pouch, breaking free of the umbilical cord. Once in, it gropes for a teat on which to feed, using well-developed sucking muscles to extract a maximum of the elaborately complex milk supply from the mother marsupial. This milk varies according to the growing infant's nutritional needs and ability to digest complex molecules. The mother's nipples swell with the stimulation, locking the connection between mother and infant. Safely secured to his food station, the tiny pademelon remains there for his first months. His chances of survival now appear to be good.

MILKY WAYS

For the Tasmanian pademelon, like other mammals, the breast's offer of nourishment, protection, and warmth is the core of the mother-infant bond.

*Crocodilians have
a special soft-lipped
smile for their
young and use
their mouths to
care for them.*

MERCURIAL GENDER

The female Nile crocodile buries her eggs in the banks of muddy rivers and sits vigilant there for twelve weeks, fending off enemies. When the eggs are agitating and making loud squawking sounds, she digs open the nest. Oddly, sex in crocodilians is determined by temperature. Females influence the sex of their offspring by moving the eggs to cooler or warmer spots. Those incubated below 86 degrees hatch into females; if the mercury rises to over 93, they hatch as males. As the hatchlings struggle into the sunlight, the female crocodile nibbles them gingerly into her mouth, stuffing a clutch of eighty or more by scooping down her tongue to create a rounded pouch. She then waddles into the shallows, slowly swishing her head from side to side till the babies drift out for their fledgling swims back to the shore. The father crocodile may act as midwife in this birthing process, first rolling the near-bursting, ready-to-go eggs on his tongue until the infants erupt, then ferrying them to the riverbank. In nature, sometimes the most savage and fearsome species can make the most affectionate parents.

*Their champion
fecundity could
fill the world with
rabbits in record
time, giving Genesis's
exhortation "Be
fruitful and multiply"
new meaning.*

FUR LININGS

Female relations of Peter Cottontail may produce up to a dozen Floppsys and Moppsys per litter while breeding throughout the year. If a female cottontail's broods all lived and reproduced, she could at the end of five years have established an empire of two-and-a-half million bunnies. Hares and rabbits differ in the way they bear and raise their young. Hares build no nest at all; they simply scrape out a small hole in the soil. Rabbits, on the other hand, often build elaborate nests carefully lined with grass and fur that the mother plucks from her underbelly. While baby hares are born fully furred, and ready to move around, newborn rabbits are born naked, blind, and so helpless that they must be cared for in a nest. One similarity between these long-eared cousins is in their response when numbers threaten plague proportions. Under unfavorable conditions of nutrition or environment, the embryos in the uterus of the female mysteriously fail to develop, and they are reabsorbed by the mother's body. Oddly, she behaves as if she has given birth, though she clearly has not. It is one of nature's intricate ways of fighting overpopulation.

POIGNANT PAIRINGS

*Named after the
Greek hero Diomedes,
whose companions
were all turned into
birds, the great
family of albatross
(Diomedeidae)
wander the world,
but always circle
back toward home.*

Albatross followed the ships of Magellan by moonlight, and today roam the waters from Antarctica to the Bering Sea, but as parents the albatross exhibit a capacity for remarkable geographic focus. Returning every other year to the same remote islands, they rest and breed with their mates-for-life. First, the female searches for a nesting spot on the rocky cliffs, scratching out a circular trench and packing down earth and vegetation into a truncated cone three feet in diameter, with a shallow bowl at the top for her single egg. For the long months it takes to brood and then rear the fledgling young, the pair take turns hatching and feeding. In some albatross species the youngster makes its first flight after nine months. The parents feed the chick less and less often, finally voluntarily deserting it. Though the wandering albatross does not breed until the age of nine, it may have a lifespan of thirty or more years, returning steadfastly to its mate to renew the family bond.

All elephant society is a complex weaving of relations. The core of the herd is a flexible family group ranging from two individuals to several dozen closely related females and young males. Males usually leave the family when they reach puberty, and thereafter they live alone or in loose temporary associations with other bulls. The birth of a new elephant calf is a family event, accompanied by much general commotion. Elephant calves enjoy a long childhood, lasting until about twelve years of age, during which they are the center of attention for the whole group. Nurturing the calves is a collective responsibility. Lactating females occasionally share their milk with a calf belonging to a sister or aunt, and subadult females take turns keeping an eye on the infant elephants. This surrogate mothering, as it actually is called, is an example of behavior motivated by kin selection, a genetic predisposition to protect the genes one shares with brothers and sisters and other close relatives.

Elephants live in a female world, a matriarchy ruled by the oldest and toughest grande dame in each herd, all busy indulging the smallest among them.

A LITTLE BUNDLE OF JOY

Family life among
the seals is based
not only on the
mating relationship,
but on the
requirements of
birth and child care.

THE FATHER FACTOR

At the beginning of the breeding season, fur seal bulls appear at Alaska's Pribilof Islands, followed one month later by females migrating three thousand miles from warmer waters south. As each cow approaches the coast, she is welcomed with a great flurry and bustle, as lone bulls try to impress cows to join their harem. Cows tend to prefer the tallest, biggest, and most popular bull so their calves will be fathered by a strong male. After winning his harem the bull must wait while his females first give birth to the offspring conceived in the spring, then suckle the young, and gradually accustom them to the water. The bull's sole concern is not to lose his wives and children, so while the mothers play about with their calves, teaching them to swim, the bull sits enthroned for four months, not eating, and using up his stock of blubber. He watches over his numerous band (which for a mature ten-year old bull can number over fifty cows and calves), offering his children an example of dignified paternity.

LIKE MOTHER, LIKE CHILD

Oviedo y Valdes,
Spanish chronicler of
the New World, wrote
that he had never
seen a more useless
creature than the
forest-loving sloth.
With fine irony, his
fellow conquistadors
named it "nimble
Peter."

Although the sloth is renowned for its glacial slowness of movement, it ranks among the most spectacularly successful large mammals in South America; its sluggish, arboreal, leaf-eating way of life is almost impervious to both competitors and predators. Sloths' rounded heads with flattened faces have small ears hidden in very short, fine underfur. An overcoat of coarser hair is grooved in moist conditions with a greenish algae, which offers camouflage in the tree canopy. All sloths have enormous stomachs where meals digest for more than a month, accounting for a third of their body weight. Breeding at any time of the year, after a six-month gestation a sloth bears its offspring in a tree and helps it to reach the teat. The infant sloth nurses for a month and rides with its mother for eight more months, hanging on with long curving claws that hook over the tree branches and feeding on convenient leaves. The baby shrills a whistling "ai-ai" sound if the mother leaves for a minute. After weaning, the young inherit their mothers' feeding range along with her taste for certain leaves. The advantage in this specialization is that several other sloths can share the range without competing for food.

On the lookout

for danger, a

meerkat from

Africa's Kalahari

Desert may be

the mother of

the babies or

just a helper.

Living in groups of about thirty, meerkats share familial responsibilities from baby-sitting to standing sentry, a system of cooperation that helps to protect the young from predators. Meerkat babies are picky eaters, and when their mother brings them food, carrying it in her mouth, a strange pantomime ensues as she leaps around in front of the babies until they follow her example, taking the food in their own mouths. Meerkats will, however, eat animal and vegetable foods of the most varied kinds. In addition, they get "food jealous" and try to grab food from the jaws of others. When the mother brings food and then incites her offspring to take it, she is actually teaching them a valuable survival lesson: which foods are suitable.

THE BABY-SITTER

Many species of
cuckoo have
managed to make
infant care simple—
by tricking other
birds into raising
their young.

SPECKLED EGGS IN A STRANGE NEST

Aristotle reported witnessing cuckoo cuckoldry in his *History of Animals* in the fifth century B.C. In the ninth century A.D. Hrabanus Maurus added to cuckoo lore, noting that a cuckoo will steal into a nest and dispose of the eggs of its involuntary host, substituting its own. For centuries the mystery of how the cuckoo managed to have its eggs resemble the unsuspecting victim's in size, color, and marking was debated. Darwin hypothesized that once upon a time cuckoos laid eggs in whatever nest was available and, gradually, a special sort of selection "for the resemblance of the egg" came about. The cuckoos all looked alike as birds, but different groups with penchants for different foster parents developed special colorings of their eggs. One other mystery has been solved. Observers noted that once cuckoos hatch, all but one nestling mysteriously vanishes. Recent films unveil the unwitting murderer. Naked and blind, the biggest cuckoo hatched possesses an urge to toss from the nest everything it finds, until every egg or other baby bird is gone. In four days, the deadly impulse is over. Oddly, the hoodwinked foster parents don't even seem to notice.

Opossums' white faces, dark gray fur, and black eye patches are familiar to North Americans; in fact they are the only marsupial north of Mexico. One of the most prolific parents of the animal world, the Virginia opossum gives birth only thirteen days after breeding to as many as fifty-six young at a time. But the attrition rate is high: the mother opossum has only thirteen teats, twelve arranged in a horseshoe arc around the thirteenth in the center. The size of bees at birth, the babies use their strong forearms to drag themselves along their mother's fur and into her pouch, where they each avidly attach themselves to a free nipple. These successful offspring spend eight weeks drinking their fill, then blinkingly emerge to spend a month piggybacking on mother as she forages for much-needed food. In this stage she begins to teach her offspring the possum's time-honored technique of survival—dropping instantly into a tight ball, feigning death for hours if necessary, even defecating to produce a convincing odor of carrion.

"Playing possum" has entered the vocabulary, a nod to the superior acting ability of the mild-mannered little marsupial formally called the opossum.

A BAKER'S DOZEN

Sisterhood exists in the animal world as well as in the bosom of the feminist movement; female giraffes with young to guard sensed that it was more economical to pool energies.

COOLING CRÈCHES

Misunderstood for generations, giraffes are "hider" ungulates that leave their young, traveling long distances without them in search of the daily hundred pounds of foliage they need to consume. This practice earned them a reputation as delinquent mothers. But recently scientists proved that giraffes leave their offspring in cool, grassy places and visit them daily to allow them to suckle. After about a month they introduce them to groups where a pair of other females acts like baby-sitters, allowing most of the mothers to browse for leaves while the surrogates stand guard. If a baby-sitter senses danger, she moves her own calf toward safety and the others follow. The crucial reason for this arrangement is thermal. The giraffe's extreme physiological construction involves an internal regulating mechanism that allows it to control temperature in its eighteen-foot body, but that has effect only after about the first year of life. To prevent junior from succumbing to sunstroke, the giraffe evolved this sophisticated day-care solution.

The olive baboons (a name which refers to the dark-green cast of their grizzle-gray coats) are among the most social of primates. In large troops of a hundred or so in the East African highlands, they travel, feed, eat, and sleep huddled together at night as a family. The matrilineal nature of baboon society is the glue in the group; the males voluntarily leave to join other groups as they near adulthood. For the male, bonding with a new family begins at the nursery. A stray male drifting in has only one route to acceptance—he must cultivate a mother and child and become their protector. He sets about it assiduously, making friendly faces, smacking his lips, and if the baby (and later the mother) permits, grooming them. If his strategy works, it provides a passport as he gradually builds relations with the relatives. Even during pregnancy or nursing, the female keeps her special friends (often two or three males), who help feed and care for the youngster. Acceptance of each male is based on his willingness and capability to make a good surrogate dad—and one who fails the test is unceremoniously ousted from the troop.

FATHERS KNOW BEST

Once it was thought that sexual attraction kept baboons together, but now mother-baby bonds are believed to be at the heart of the matter.

NIP AND TUCK

*Wolf packs are
essentially nuclear
families, defined
by a dominant
"alpha" pair, male
and female, and
subordinate wolves
that are either their
younger siblings
or their offspring.*

Alpha wolves are leaders of the pack and make all important decisions, including where to find food and water. In May, the alpha female prepares a den, and three weeks later she gives birth to five pups, licking each one clean as she pushes it free, eating the afterbirth and cord. The newborns are dark balls of fur, blind and deaf—but in a mere three weeks they are able to gambol in the spring sunshine. Pups bond quickly to any wolf who pays attention to them, and all the pack shows an abundance of tolerance. While the alpha female nurses her pups, the others in the pack hunt, eating at the kill site and bringing food home in their stomachs. Pups greet the returning adults with gleeful nips on their mouths and the wolves regurgitate the semidigested meat so that the pups can devour it. As the summer goes by, the alpha female begins to join in the hunt. A young female then becomes a baby-sitter for the pups. Her motives are not disinterested; by bonding closely with the alpha pups she can raise her status in the pack, while protecting the genes that she shares with them.

One of the world's
largest owls, the
great gray shelters
her owlets, hatched
a few days apart,
in the darkened
branches of northern
coniferous forests.

Come breeding time, the gray male owl courts the female by offering her a beakful of food. Through this gesture the male proves that he can provide food for the family, for the female while nesting, and for the offspring when they hatch. Around mid-February the two mates look for a nesting site, and in March or April the female lays an average of three or four eggs. After about thirty days, the owlets hatch, white and helpless but equipped with special white egg teeth to help in extracting themselves from the shell. It is two months before they can take their first flights. During that time, the mother sits patiently on the nest guarding her offspring, and the male provides the food; often he perches in a nearby branch waiting for the mother to signal with a chirping sound that she or the young are hungry. Then he flies away and returns with lunch for everyone.

MOONLIT FEATHERED NEST

Small, agile, and inquisitive, the squirrel monkey soars through the branches of the forest, "flying" from limb to limb in an electric blur of motion.

TRAPEZE ARTISTS

In the remote Amazon jungles, several hundred monkeys peer suddenly from the foliage, cocking their heads as they swing down for a vantage point. Such inquisitiveness starts just after birth, in the month when young infants ride their mothers' backs. Afterward they venture off to play for increasing hours each day. During this exploration period, the young monkey learns how to close its fist on flying insects, how to open various fruits, where the water holes are, and where the safe arboreal pathways are found. Play is important, giving the baby a chance to develop skills for running and jumping through the branches, which is crucial if it is to evade a hawk. Play also helps perfect social skills with peers and adults in the family, as well as a monkey's form in fighting: wrestling, sparring, feinting, pouncing, and dodging. As much as play is fun, it helps wean the child from its mother, so that by twelve months, an infant spends nearly all its time with its age-mates. Soon, other interests hold sway: cuddling, care of infants, and sexual interactions—all involving skills formed in that crucial nursery in the treetops.

Despite the Antarctic cold, penguins breed in seeming bliss on niches in the rocks or in holes dug in the shelves of ice extending out to the sea. Flocking to the rookeries, the females lay their eggs in May for fall hatching, marking the nest with a circle of stones. Mother departs to the sea and the male takes over, balancing the precious egg on the tops of his feet and pulling down his feathery pouch to shield it from the bitter cold. If his mate hasn't returned by the time the baby is born, he single-handedly feeds the hatched chick, covered in its thick coat of down, with a high-protein, richly caloric liquid secreted by his esophageal sac. In the process, the male penguin can lose up to half his body weight. Once the chicks are strong enough to fend for themselves, they matriculate in giant "kindergartens" where parents care collectively for all the young. When they are old enough to shed their down for the slicker adult plumage, they spend four formative years learning to swim and fish in schools. Meanwhile, the father penguin returns to the sea to feed and fatten up for the next year's grueling parenting session. His offspring will inherit the empire of ice.

LOVE ON THE ROCKS

Waist high to man, the emperor penguin is the largest in the world, and perhaps the hardiest.

Ideal examples of the sacrifices of motherhood, polar bear females only mate every three years, and so each of their cubs is deeply precious.

VANILLA ICE

When the fall arrives the pregnant polar bear looks for a place to den, normally far from the sea and well protected against the wind. Gestation takes six to ten weeks, during which she hibernates, without eating or drinking. After her two or three cubs are born she doesn't leave the den for the two months that they are utterly helpless, needing her heat and milk in order to survive. Polar bear milk is the richest in fat among mammals, a magic elixir that enables the cubs to double their weight in two weeks. By the time they grow to twelve pounds the cubs begin to explore in and around the den, even though their mother is still in a lethargic state. In early spring they finally emerge. Mother lies lazily at the entrance of the den while the cubs play. For the next two years, she is not only the food provider but also guide, teacher, and protector, leading them over the ice floes as they travel toward the sea in order to find food.

ACKNOWLEDGMENTS

Grateful thanks to Lala Herrero Salas, whose tireless research provided the raw material in the early stages of the project. We would also like to thank Vanessa Ryan for her elegant design and endless grace under pressure. Many thanks also to friends and colleagues for their knowledge, time, and patience in the research process, including Les Kaufman, Chief Scientist, Edgerton Research Lab, New England Aquarium, for his ruthless and peerless vetting of all the material here; Gonzalo Escuder of New York University; Bill Perry from National Geographic; Tim Harris from NHPA; Ben Rose from The National Zoo; Douglas B. Smith from Boston Museum of Science; Bill Holmstrom, Jamie James, Steve Johnson, Peter Taylor and Roseanne Thiemann from Wildlife Conservation International at the New York Zoological Society; Dennis Thoney and Paul Sieswerda from W.C.I. at the New York Aquarium; Jonathan David of Tulip Films; and Andy Karsch of Longfellow Pictures. Very special thanks to Caroline Herter of Chronicle Books, as well as Charlotte Stone, Carey Charlesworth, and Fonda Duvanel, who took such a keen interest in this project and without whose many suggestions and unwavering enthusiasm this book would have hibernated forever.

PICTURE CREDITS